Disney

MICKEY MOUSE CLUBHOUSE

Illustrated by Sue DiCicco and the Disney Storybook Art Team

phoenix international publications, inc.

Meeska. Mooska. Mickey Mouse! Welcome to the Clubhouse! It's time for roll call. Can you find these friends?

Minnie

Pluto

Mickey

Goofy

Donald

Daisy

Spring-cleaning makes Donald sneeze—and he bumps right into the April Shower Maker! Look for things that will help the friends tidy up:

spray bottle

duster

sponge

dustpan

bucket

broom

mop

The spring from the April Shower Maker bounced away! Without rain, the plants will need water. Look for these things that hold water:

thermos

bird bath

canteen

water balloon

cactus

fish bowl

watering can

Mickey spots the spring at a trampoline farm, and Toodles is ready to help with new Mouseketools. Look for these tools from past adventures:

toolbox

glue stick

shoes

skis

ribbon

thermometer

The spring bounced up a trampoline stalk! Balloons from Toodles can help. As Mickey and Goofy float up, up, up, look for these cloud shapes in the sky:

HELLO, MICKEY!

Willie the Giant thinks the spring is a toy. While Mickey trades a bouncy ball from Toodles for the spring, find some of Willie's other giant-sized toys:

train

doll

fire truck

pinwheel

bike

pogo stick

rocking horse

The Mystery Mouseketool, a parachute, brings the friends back home. Now the April Shower Maker is fixed! Find these friends who came to celebrate:

What's different?

Can you see what's different? Look for 10 differences between each pair of pictures. Check the answer key on the next page!

Mickey and his pals grow beautiful flowers. Visit the garden again to count flowers of these different colors and patterns:

1 rainbow flower
2 pink polka-dot flowers
3 blue checkered flowers
4 yellow striped flowers
5 pink flowers
6 bunches of green star flowers
7 purple zigzag flowers
8 red heart flowers

Minnie loves springtime. She even loves the word spring! Go back to spring-cleaning day and look for things that rhyme with spring:

ring
string
wing
king
swing

Birds love to visit the birdbath in the garden. Fly back for a little bird-watching. Can you find these special birds?

red-headed woodpecker

blue-throated hummingbird

pink-footed goose

little blue heron

white-winged scoter

green kingfisher

black-winged stilt

Mickey, Minnie, Mousekedoer, and Mouseketool all start with the letter M. Can you find some more things that start with the letter M?

mailbox	medal
map	microscope
mug	math book
milk	marbles

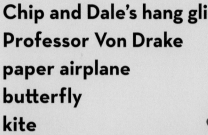

Mickey and Goofy flew to the trampoline farm to try to catch the runaway spring. Float back to see what else can fly:

Chip and Dale's hang glider
Professor Von Drake
paper airplane
butterfly
kite

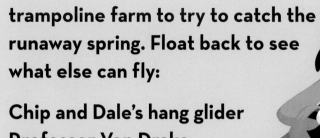

Willie the Giant loves to play baseball, but he can't find equipment his own size. Look for these objects the creative giant uses instead:

telephone pole (baseball bat)
water tower (tee and baseball)
fishing boats and fish net (baseball mitt)
a house (home plate)
parking lot (first base)
golf green (second base)
billboard (third base)

Now that the April Shower Maker is working, the vegetable garden can grow! See if you can find all of these healthy vegetables:

tomatoes
lettuce
carrots
cucumbers
corncobs
broccoli
celery

What's different?

Answer Key